JOURNEY
OF THE
PRODIGAL

Also by Brennan Manning

Ruthless Trust

Abba's Child

The Signature of Jesus

Reflections for Ragamuffins

The Ragamuffin Gospel

Lion and Lamb

A Stranger to Self-Hatred

Souvenirs of Solitude

The Wisdom of Accepted Tenderness

The Gentle Revolutionaries

Prophets and Lovers

BRENNAN MANNING

JOURNEY
OF THE
PRODIGAL

*A Parable of
Sin and Redemption*

A Crossroad Carlisle Book
The Crossroad Publishing Company
New York • Berkeley

The Crossroad Publishing Company
481 Eighth Avenue, Suite 1550
New York, NY 10001

Printed in the United States of America

Library of Congress Cataloging-in-Publication Data

Manning, Brennan.
    Journey of the prodigal : a parable of sin and
redemption / Brennan Manning.
      p. cm.
    "A Crossroad Carlisle book".
    ISBN 0-8245-2014-9 (alk. paper)
    1. Redemption – Fiction.   I. Title. II. Series.
PS3563.A5365 J68 2003
813'.54 – dc21

                       2002013456

1 2 3 4 5 6 7 8 9 10   08 07 06 05 04 03 02

A Parable of
Sin and Redemption

Orphaned as a young child, Willie Juan lived with his loving grandmother, Calm Sunset, in the poor Mexican village of Hopi on the banks of the Rio Grande.

With his Irish, African, Asian, Spanish, Indian, and Mexican ancestry, Willie Juan had an unusual complexion and bright copper-colored hair. An early childhood accident left him with a crooked leg, a limp, and a body full of scars. So, although he was a kind, inquisitive little boy, he was taunted by the village children, who made fun of the way he looked.

"Speckled trout!" they'd yell. "Speckled trout!"

While the children's cruelty hurt Willie Juan, at home the little boy was deeply loved by his grandmother, who always told him stories of Jesus, whom she called El Shaddai, and how He loved His people, especially children like Willie Juan.

He took comfort in those stories, as his grandmother held him and rocked him to sleep.

One hot summer day, saddened by not

having any friends, Willie Juan went to the village church, looking for the peace he'd always found there.

Seeing the wooden statue of El Shaddai, with His kind, sad, gentle eyes, Willie Juan stopped and stared in wonder. In such heat, Willie Juan thought, He must be thirsty.

The little boy got a cup of water, went back to the Man on the Cross, and gave Him a drink. As Willie Juan poured the cool water into the statue's half-open mouth, the water ran down His painted chin and onto the altar.

Just then, the priest ran in, saw what Willie Juan had done, and scolded the little boy for pouring water on the wooden statue.

Willie Juan did not understand. He thought he was helping El Shaddai by giving Him a cool drink. Why was the priest mad at him? Willie Juan was too young to understand about such things as the effect of water on painted wood.

As he left the church, he quickly forgot about the priest's lecture, but he couldn't stop thinking about El Shaddai, with His beautiful, sad eyes.

Journey of the Prodigal

Throughout the fall, Willie Juan looked forward to the village's joyful fiesta of the Virgin of Guadalupe, which would be celebrated in December. He saved what he'd earned by caring for the village donkey, and when the day finally came, he set out to enjoy the fiesta, especially the children's carnival and delicious foods, not knowing that this day would change his life.

At the fiesta, he walked through a swirl of music and laughter, colorful costumes, and the aroma of his favorite foods. As he was deciding whether to buy a tortilla or a juicy fajita, he saw an old wagon hitched to a horse. The sign on the wagon said, "The Great Medicine Show."

Willie Juan wandered into the crowd in front of the wagon and saw a tall, gaunt stranger who called himself the Medicine Man. When Willie Juan saw the man about to speak to the crowd, he looked at his sad, gentle, kind, piercing eyes and recognized instantly that the Medicine Man was El Shaddai.

The Medicine Man looked across the crowd and directly at Willie Juan. As he smiled at the little boy, the Medicine Man's eyes sparkled with joy. Instead of addressing the crowd, the Medicine Man took Willie Juan aside.

"I have been waiting for you," he told the little boy.

Willie Juan wasn't used to people being happy to see him.

The Medicine Man cried tears of compassion for Willie Juan's scars and crooked leg. He talked about love and healing. He offered to share his lunch with Willie Juan.

While they ate, Willie Juan told him about losing his parents, living with his devoted grandmother, and how he wished he had a friend.

"Willie Juan, I am your friend," the Medicine Man answered.

Willie Juan was ecstatic. He had a friend! His first friend, and it was El Shaddai.

Since Willie Juan had never had a friend before, he asked the Medicine Man what it meant to be a friend. The little boy feared he might not know how to be one and might disappoint him.

So El Shaddai taught Willie Juan about friendship. There is no friendship without love, the Medicine Man explained, no matter what else you have between you. A friend is always patient with you, kind to you, never jealous of your other friends, never rude, never uses you, and is always forgiving.

He taught the boy that friendship is based on three things: faith in your friend, hope for your friend, and, most importantly, the love of your friend.

As your friend, El Shaddai told Willie Juan, "I will never fail you."

He taught Willie Juan about forgiveness of others, acceptance of self, and joy.

Self-acceptance, he explained, is an act of trust in God the Father, whom El Shaddai called Abba. "When the Spirit of El Shaddai comes upon you," he said, "then you will be healed."

Willie Juan wanted so much to be healed.

"Accept in faith, never doubting," the Medicine Man instructed. "Ask and you will receive, seek and you will find, knock and the door will open to you."

He thanked Willie Juan for the drink of water the little boy gave the statue of El Shaddai in the church. "I will never for-

17

get it," El Shaddai said. "It will not go unrewarded."

It was time for the Medicine Man to leave. He smiled, blessed Willie Juan, and rode off to the west.

Willie Juan skipped and sang all the way home. When he told his grandmother about his encounter with El Shaddai, she told him he must go to the Cave of Bright Darkness in the nearby mountains, a holy retreat of solitude often used by pilgrims. The local villagers believed that you could meet El Shaddai in the Cave of Bright Darkness.

Willie Juan hiked up the mountain to the cave. Inside, he found granite walls, cool air, and an altar.

After a storm raged outside, Willie Juan heard a voice that spoke of surrendering in unwavering trust to El Shaddai. After the Voice's teachings, El Shaddai entered the cave.

Willie Juan ran to him with joy.

El Shaddai taught the little boy that to be El Shaddai's friend and understand his teachings, he had to trust him unconditionally, for that kind of trust is the "seal of friendship."

He taught Willie Juan about forgiveness, and about the courage it takes to accept El Shaddai's acceptance and love.

Willie Juan was eager to accept him and to learn. He hugged the Medicine Man pleading, "El Shaddai, my Friend, please don't leave me and don't ever let me leave you."

"I will never leave you," El Shaddai reassured him, and he instructed the little boy to go to the altar. He blessed Willie Juan and left the cave.

Willie Juan stood before the altar, stunned as his leg and scars were healed.

Healed, he was healed!

Willie Juan wept tears of joy as he cried, "Abba, Abba, Abba!"

Running out of the cave and down the mountain, he cried, "Abba, I belong to You," as he made his way home and into the waiting arms of his grandmother.

The boy who cried "Abba!" had joyously returned home to his village, his crooked leg and scars healed in the Cave of Bright Darkness by El Shaddai.

The villagers gathered in front of Willie Juan's house. His healing caused quite a stir for a while in the village of Hopi, but soon life went on as before for the little boy.

Journey of the Prodigal

Years went by and Willie Juan finished grade school without distinction. His marks were very ordinary. Though he studied hard, he just couldn't seem to remember what he read, especially the long answers in his religion classes.

One day in the sixth grade, his teacher, Sister Mary Isabel, asked the class, "Who is Jesus Christ?"

She expected the standard catechism definition. "He is the union of two natures in one Divine Person."

Willie Juan shot up his hand. That surprised everyone, and it shocked the teacher.

"Yes, Willie Juan" said Sister Mary Isabel. "He's the son of Abba Dabba, sister." Willie Juan got three days detention.

He tried sports but wasn't coordinated. He auditioned for the choir but was told that he sang like a frog calling hogs. He flunked out as an altar boy because he rang the bell when he should have brought the book, and he shouted "Alleluia" any time it seemed like the right thing to do.

After school, Willie Juan loved to whittle with his penknife. What a gift he had with

25

wood! An ugly stick or a block of wood took shape, contour, and form under the magic of the blade in his long, sinewy hands.

The neighbors marveled. They didn't expect anything like this from Willie Juan. Once he worked for three whole weeks breathing life into a dead piece of wood and then presented it to his grandmother, Calm Sunset. It was the face of Jesus. She stared in disbelief, her eyes filled with tears.

"Willie Juan," she said, "He almost seems alive."

"He is, Grandmother."

"Why is He smiling?" she asked. "It's

not really a smile," Willie Juan said, "It is a grin. He grins a lot and His eyes twinkle. Sometimes He throws back His head and He laughs and laughs and He makes me laugh too."

It was Willie Juan's grandmother who first told him about Jesus, whom she also called El Shaddai. When Willie Juan was a child, Clam Sunset would rock him to sleep with stories of El Shaddai, and how much He loved His people. He especially loved children. They ran to Him whenever they saw Him and never wanted to leave Him.

27

Calm Sunset told Willie Juan that El Shaddai was as compassionate as He was powerful. El Shaddai was the most loving Friend anyone could have.

Willie Juan had found this out for himself when he'd met the Medicine Man at the fiesta of the Virgin of Guadalupe.

Almost immediately, Willie Juan realized that the Medicine Man was really El Shaddai. It was His eyes. So intense, yet so calm and loving. The Medicine Man knew that Willie Juan recognized that He was El Shaddai.

The Medicine Man became Willie Juan's

first real friend. But this Friend would be different from all the others he would meet in his lifetime.

This Friend was the Son of Abba, the Father.

With his grandmother's encouragement, Willie Juan went to a vocational and technical school to study woodcrafting. Within a short time even the teacher began to learn from his astonishing pupil.

Money for life's necessities was scarce in Hopi. Suddenly, there was none at all. Heavy rains destroyed the soybean crops and unemployment was rampant.

Upon graduation, though his grandmother fussed a little, Willie Juan told her that he had to leave to find work but would come back in a few months with money.

He slipped across the Laredo River under cover of darkness, eluded the border patrol, and made his way to the house of a Hopi migrant worker who was now living in the big city. The migrant workers welcomed him and got him a menial job in the barrio.

His wood carvings quickly attracted attention. A merchant volunteered to sell them in his store. One day, a wealthy tourist spotted a carving of a small lamb.

"This is a masterpiece," he cried. "Who is the artist?"

Willie Juan suddenly found himself transported to Santa Fe, New Mexico, living in a mansion and commissioned to carve a bust of José Antonio Luis, an aesthetic millionaire and patron of the arts.

One afternoon, at a lavish lawn party for Santa Fe's aristocracy, the bust was unveiled.

The crowd gasped, "Awesome! Stunning! Life-like resemblance! Who is the artist?"

Suddenly, commissions rolled in for Willie Juan, along with thousands and thousands of dollars. He bought a home, arranged for his grandmother's trip to Santa Fe, and then went to the eye doctor because his eyes wouldn't stop watering.

At Mass one Sunday, the priest talked about God's love for the poor. Willie Juan left church and went directly to the barrio and gave away a lot of money. He stopped at a corner where a girl of about eighteen was selling watermelons and bubble gum. Willie Juan stared. She was thin, wore a sack dress, and looked like a pathetic little urchin. But oh, her face. Her deep brown eyes shimmered with compassion; her nose perked with pride; her mouth was a bubbling brook. Her countenance was radiantly beautiful.

Then a fat Anglo customer with a ruby in his right ear and a fifty-dollar bill in his hand approached and said to the girl, "Whisper something dirty in my ear and this fifty is yours."

She lowered her eyes and said softly, "Oh, no sir, I would never do that."

The man snorted, screamed obscenities at her, and stormed off.

"A heaven full of stars is not as beautiful as what I just saw," Willie Juan said to himself. He bought all of the melons and the bubble gum, found out that her name was Ana, and asked if he might come to see her that night.

Ana lived in grinding poverty and heart-rending squalor. The little cardboard shack she called home was only eight feet long. Yet it was brightly colored and spotlessly clean. It was always filled with little children who seemed to have nowhere else to go.

Willie Juan was moved not just by Ana's beauty — he had seen pretty girls before and had never reacted like this — but by something that seemed to radiate from deep inside her soul.

It entered his open heart and warmed his entire being.

It was pure love.

He remembered that life-changing day in the Cave of Bright Darkness when he was a child and El Shaddai healed Willie Juan's crooked leg and scars. El Shaddai told him that Abba, the Father, wants His children "to live with passion in the beauty of the moment, accepting and enjoying His gifts."

Was Ana a gift from God?

Willie Juan thought so.

Everyone who knew her would have agreed.

On their second date, he had asked to take her up to his house for an afternoon or evening visit, but she would not agree to it, and he didn't understand why anyone would turn down such comfort. Perhaps, he thought, it's too soon. When she knows me better, she will agree to visit my home.

Ana and Willie Juan saw each other every day for a week. Each afternoon, he bought the fruit and candies Ana had to sell so he could take her away from the streets for a while.

They took long walks and then sat by the

river as Willie Juan worked with a piece of wood to create her radiant face.

Ana was moved by Willie Juan's talent and by how he saw her as he revealed her spirit in his creation.

Willie Juan told Ana all about his childhood in the Mexican village of Hopi, first living with his mother and father, who worked so hard in the fields, then taken in by his beloved grandmother, Calm Sunset, after he was orphaned.

He told her about his mixed heritage, which explained his bright copper-colored hair and unusual complexion, and how the village children teased him for it, and for the physical scars and disfigured leg he had received as a toddler in a car accident.

While he told her that a mysterious Medicine Man healed his leg and made his scars disappear, he didn't mention that the Medicine Man was El Shaddai — Jesus. Willie Juan just wasn't sure how Ana might react to hearing such a story. She might think he was crazy. He decided he'd wait a while before telling her the whole story.

Every evening she asked him to take her back to her makeshift home in the barrio so she could look after all the children who would wander in at dusk. They were orphaned or abandoned, and always welcome. Ana made room for as many as the room would hold and fed them whatever she could.

Her task was made easier on those days of Willie Juan's visits.

On the way back to her home each evening, they always stopped in the marketplace, and Willie Juan bought more food for the evening than Ana could have bought in an entire month.

Together they'd carry it back to Ana's,

and then the older children would help her prepare the evening meal for all of them, except Willie Juan.

He always left after helping to bring in the baskets of food. He just couldn't bring himself to stay in this wretched place any longer than he had to.

It broke his heart to see Ana living in such squalor.

Willie Juan vowed to himself, "One day I will take Ana away from the poverty of this barrio."

He told his grandmother about Ana, and she was happy. "What is her last name?"

she asked. "I don't know," he replied. "I just never asked."

"Please bring her home one day."

"Sí, Grandmother."

The following night, Willie Juan walked hand in hand with Ana along the riverbank. She had fallen in love with him, too. He was kind and gentle, honest and uncomplicated.

Suddenly, Willie Juan stopped. "Ana, I love you with all my heart, and I am asking you to marry me. I will take you away from the barrio to live in my spacious house high on the hill, with running water and a flower garden and a bathtub."

"Oh, Willie Juanito," she said, using her pet name for him. "I love you too, and I am so honored that you want me to be yours, but I could never leave the barrio. My heart is with my people."

Willie Juan's jaw dropped. "You mean to marry you I must live like you in a little cardboard shack with no water and no bathtub? I have worked so hard to get away from all this."

Her eyes said it all, "I am sorry, Willie Juanito."

Willie Juan went home that night torn up inside. "I can't go back," he screamed into the night. "I can't go back there, never, never."

Clutching his half-completed wood carving of Ana, he moped around the house for weeks. His vision was blurred, but he thought it was because he had cried so much. His grandmother tried, but nothing she said or did could console him.

Then, came a knock at the door, it was Ana's younger brother, Migalito. Ana had been run over by a car. She had died an hour before.

Willie Juan sank to the floor as if an arrow had pierced his heart.

The police arrested a fat, drunken Anglo with a ruby in his right ear and charged him with manslaughter. Willie Juan was enraged. He cried out, he screamed, "Why didn't El Shaddai, the Medicine Man, do something to stop that crazy man?"

Grief-stricken, he dragged himself to the funeral mass and out to the cemetery. His sight was deteriorating rapidly. So the pastor read him the inscription on her tombstone. "Here lies Ana Wim, God's little one."

When the priest explained the tradition in the Bible of the "Ana Wim," the long line of Israel's little ones who loved the poor and being poor, and had unfailing trust in God Willie Juan was racked with guilt and even more grief. At home, he was inconsolable.

Unfortunately, his grandmother had to leave suddenly for Hopi because her best friend was terminally ill.

Willie Juan knew that his grandmother was doing the right thing. And besides, he thought, it didn't really matter whether she was home with him or not, since he didn't respond to her attempts to comfort him.

He could hardly see now, and when he held his wood carving of Ana's beautiful face in his hands, he had to see it in his mind's eye. When he looked at the carving, he only saw a blur.

First he lost his beloved Ana, and now this.

Alone and lonely, his heart ready to break with sorrow, Willie Juan roamed the house bumping into chairs and tables. Two weeks after Ana Wim's death, he went totally blind. The doctors used big words like "progressive deterioration of the retina."

Since arriving in Santa Fe, Willie Juan's memory of the Medicine Man had been steadily fading into the distance, long before his sight began to fade. He'd been so caught up in career, romance, recognition, prosperity, and taking a bath every day that he simply hadn't found the time for luxuries like God and His Son, El Shaddai. "And now," he demanded, "where were You when that madman struck down my Ana? Where were You? And where are You now?"

Getting no answers, he turned to tequila. He stumbled around the house with his cane, drunk most of the time, always refusing to answer the door and the telephone. He felt guilty about Ana, about preferring comfort and nice things to her love.

When he chose not to see Ana, he hadn't thought about El Shaddai's teachings about love. He hadn't asked for His help, or Abba's either.

Although Willie Juan didn't realize it, when he shut love out of his life, he was shutting out El Shaddai and Abba too.

He felt betrayed by Jesus. The depression followed the euphoria of the tequila. In the darkness of total blindness, he could no longer carve wood, Willie Juan sank into utter hopelessness and despair.

In the cave, El Shaddai had told Willie Juan about times of despair and loss of faith: "When some people feel that they have been abandoned by El Shaddai, when their lives fill with loneliness, rejection, failure, and depression, when they are deaf to everything but the shriek of their own pain, then their trust in El Shaddai vanishes as quickly as last night's dream."

Willie Juan remembered none of that now as he lived out El Shaddai's words.

Early one morning, Migalito pried open a window and crawled into Willie Juan's house. He awoke Willie Juan. "I brought you a present."

"What did you bring?" Willie Juan mumbled through swollen, puffed lips.

"Instead of drowning your pain in tequila, blow it out through this trumpet. He placed it into Willie Juan's hands.

" I love you, my friend," said Migalito. "Now go back to sleep."

Hours later, Willie Juan awakened with

his head pounding and his heart aching. He reached for the trumpet, pursed his lips, and blew. Oh, God, how he blew, how he blew! It was beautiful. He couldn't sing, he had no musical training, but in an instant the trumpet became his other self.

Pouring out his agony, he unleashed torrents of sixteen notes at blinding speed, then throttled down wistfully into the middle register of the horn in a wailing cry.

"Magic, sheer magic," cried a neighbor down the street, who owned the Santa Fe Repertory Theater.

The next week, Willie Juan's grandmother returned from Hopi and was at the theater to see him. Willie Juan opened with a five-man ensemble. He stood in the middle of the stage, his feet planted firmly on the ground, his slender frame shivering in rags. And the only sound that came screaming out of the trumpet in driving, pulsing, melodic thrusts was "Do you love me, do you love me, do you love me?" Suddenly, the five-man ensemble dropped their instruments, then backed away safely at a distance. They stared at Willie Juan because they knew that he was blowing for every one of them.

The following morning, Calm Sunset read Willie Juan the reviews. The music critic of a prestigious local newspaper wrote, "Last night, a skinny, blind, twenty-one-year-old man ambled onto the stage, hiked up his horn, and blew the roof off the repertory theater. In one dazzling performance, he did everything that has ever been done with a trumpet. This kid is going places."

Willie Juan rose to superstardom like a flaming meteor on a moonless night. He played the top stages around the world to packed houses. His stunning arrangements introduced a new era both to classical and jazz concerts. His harmonies and rhythms grew more complex, and his swiftly changing chords and furious tempos required an astonishing command of the instrument.

After two years of touring the country and the world, his hour of triumph arrived, a trumpet concert, with the full Philharmonic Orchestra in New York City.

Later that week, a prestigious magazine would report, "A ragged blind boy named Willie Juan brought the trumpet to a place that it has never been before. His glowing, rounded tones, technical precision, and fully developed sense of flow and shading were spellbinding. He swooped and slid through the full range of the horn. In the finale, when the kid hiked up his horn and flirted outrageously with the melody, climbing in counterpoint, tossing notes and nuances back and forth in the air, the heavens fell silent and Gabriel listened. The young man with the horn owns the City."

Every other major magazine and newspaper agreed, except one, which commented, "Willie Juan's self-absorption and aloofness reveals a brokenness that needs mending. An enormous talent that still needs time to ripen."

Willie Juan knew that it was the truth. His heart was empty, and that made his triumph trivial. He cancelled his upcoming world tour and withdrew into solitude. He lay awake night after night. He knew his music had fire, soul, and blues. What was missing? What was so conspicuously missing was jubilation.

Willie Juan felt like a walking shell that was once filled with personality. He still used his cane, all of his gestures moved and seemed human, but the fire inside had died. He had lost what a beloved poet called "the inward music." He was a sad twenty-three-year-old trumpeter who lived a hollow life.

He was uneasy and restless, even though he'd finally had been able to forgive the Medicine Man for Ana's tragic death. "I cannot dump the evil in man's heart on God; it's not fair to blame El Shaddai," he said to himself. He tried to talk to El Shaddai but quit, because it all seemed so artificial. The few words he spoke were forced, and they felt hollow in his empty heart. There was no joy being in the shadow of El Shaddai.

Willie Juan knew that he had failed his

best friend. Vanity and pride had blinded him. Wanting recognition, applause, and success had hardened his heart. His insensitivity to Ana shocked him. He had failed; his whole life was a disappointment to the Son of Abba. He had ruined that holy friendship through his own faults and felt powerless to undo what he had done.

It was becoming dangerous for Willie Juan to be alone, and he knew it. Since solitude can be fatal for a person who does not burn with great passion for anyone or anything, he abruptly decided to pick up his grandmother and Migalito and leave Santa Fe to spend Christmas in Hopi.

The village had changed, oh, how it had changed. The houses were freshly painted, and there was electricity, winter heat, and bathtubs. Hopi now had a food bank, a farm co-op, and brand new modern machinery to harvest the crops.

The villagers were puzzled, perplexed, in fact, bewitched, over the identity of their mystery benefactor who had paid for all of this. "Probably some rich industrialist from the north who is feeling guilty about all the people he cheated," they said.

The villagers largely ignored Willie Juan. Their famous native son had uprooted himself from home. "He's found greener pastures with wealthy gringos," they said. "He doesn't speak our language anymore."

Deeply hurt by their distance, Willie Juan buried his feelings in small talk with his grandmother, writing music, and wrapping Christmas presents he had ordered from a catalogue. His grandmother could never look at him without pain.

One morning a telegram arrived from Raphael Ramirez, the cardinal archbishop of Mexico City. It read,

> Dear Willie Juan,
>
> The people of God in Mexico City would be honored if you would share your great gift and play a trumpet medley at the midnight mass on Christmas Eve, at the stadium in Mexico City.
>
> > Sincerely in Christ,
> > His Eminence,
> > Raphael Cardinal Ramirez

Willie Juan blinked in astonishment. He read it, turning to Migalito. "Do it, little brother. God is calling you," Migalito said. "I wouldn't know what to play, said Willie Juan. Christmas is a time of joy, and my heart is so sad. It is the birthday of Jesus, and I feel like I'm going to a funeral."

"Be true to yourself, listen to your heart, play only what you hear in your heart," Migalito said, putting his hand on the sad young man's shoulder.

Meanwhile, the mayor of Hopi was splashing in his new bathtub when the telephone rang. Was it the call he had been waiting for? Yes, indeed. It was his brother-in-law, who was plant manager of a farm machinery company in the United States. "There is no doubt, I saw the signed bill of sale. Willie Juan bought all of the new farm equipment and everything else for the people of Hopi. He is your mystery benefactor," he told the mayor.

The mayor smiled. "That young man

has the heart of a lion," he said. Then he arranged for charter buses, so the whole village could go to the midnight mass in faraway Mexico City.

The outdoor stadium seated a hundred thousand people. Mexican men, who never went to church, now flocked through the turnstiles. "God," they sneered, "is only there to get you hatched, matched, and dispatched, but then he disappears. He doesn't care. He is indifferent to the goings on and the pain of his people."

Even the president was there with all of his political minions. "What an opportunity," he muttered. "Now this huge throng will know that I am a man anointed and sent by God."

The entire 150-person Cathedral Choir stood on stage, and the Philharmonic sat anxiously in the orchestra pit. The peasants of Hopi were nestled far back in the distant bleachers.

The lights dimmed. Only the stage, with a simple altar, was aglow. The maestro of the orchestra raised his baton, and a hundred thousand stadium voices broke into thunderous song with, "O Come, All Ye Faithful." The cardinal and his entourage entered in solemn procession. The mass began.

The readings pierced Willie Juan's heart. He wept when the choir sang "Silent Night, Holy Night" as a responsorial song. During the homily, the cardinal spoke softly and with deep emotion about Jesus, the child of Bethlehem. Still moved by "Silent Night, Holy Night," Willie Juan stood off in the wings, alone and lonely in the vast crowd, barely hearing a word of the homily. During the distribution of communion, he continued waiting as the Cathedral Choir launched into the triumphant

"Joy to the World." When everyone had returned to their seats, Cardinal Ramirez signaled for a quiet pause for meditation.

Cardinal Ramirez broke the silence of the completed meditation with this simple introduction: "Tonight, we are privileged to be the first to hear a song written especially for this blessed occasion by a most gifted musician and composer, Willie Juan."

Willie Juan's grandmother gasped. Migalito's eyes widened. The Hopi villagers in the massive crowd whispered to each other in pleasant surprise.

Except for the choir, no one knew that

Willie Juan had written a special song for the evening. He hadn't told a soul, not even his grandmother or Migalito. He had performed his own music before, but this was the first time Willie Juan had ever written lyrics.

They had come to him all at once, so quickly that he could hardly write them down fast enough. And now it was time to share them.

Willie Juan stepped to the podium, tears streaming down his cheeks. The mayor whispered to his wife, "Those are the tears of a blind lion."

Then, in the beautiful afterglow of holy communion, with the triumphant echo of "Joy to the World" still ringing, in the euphoria of the Christmas pageant, Willie Juan raised up his horn and blew a wrenching melody into the crisp, starlit winter night, as the chorus sang,

> My heart is broken,
> my soul is bare,
> is anyone listening,
> Does anyone care?
> Oh, long ago,
> I knew you,

in the joy of first love
we walked close together,
in company with the Dove.
Then I lost you, my friend,
when pain tore my heart.
Why weren't you listening,
when I drifted far apart?

The vast audience gasped in stunned silence. Willie Juan soared over the piano and rhythm section in long, achingly slow lines, lines that faded away into a wisp of sound more imagined than heard.

The sound of men sobbing spread

through the stadium. In the past, they had been willing to settle for a shallow Christmas, a superficial Christmas, a Christmas filled with routine prayers, well-behaved music, a whiff of euphoria, and a little overindulgence in tequila after church.

Suddenly that wasn't enough. As the skinny kid's horn mourned, flared, and stabbed, it became the cry of a wounded deer, the bleating of a lost sheep, the scream of a shipwrecked soul. Willie Juan was blowing for every one of them. They had tried to tame their desires, reduce their longings. Willie Juan's trumpet stared them in the face, exposed their hearts, and pierced them to the quick.

Haunted by the memory of the Medicine Man, Willie Juan slowed his rhythm, as the choir continued his melody of longing:

> Who will be there for me,
> who will care?
> Does anyone need me?
> Is anyone there?
> You were there
> when I needed a friend,
> you saw my soul
> when no one cared.

You showed me truth and love,
and how to soar above
the world with you at my side.

Willie Juan was lost in his music, self-absorbed in his pain. Cardinal Ramirez wept aloud and without shame. The stadium was awash in a sea of forsakenness. Then, suddenly, like a single flash of brilliant lightning across a darkened sky, a tall, gaunt, angular man stood up in the last row of seats, picked up his weatherbeaten horn, and began to blow.

Instantly, Willie Juan dropped his trumpet. He couldn't believe what he heard. No man had ever dared to hike up a horn and so stretch the limits of jazz, so push back the frontiers of classical music. It was like a scintillating sorcerer calling forth magic from every note.

The sound ricocheted off the stars. With unbearable intensity, the words gushed out of the horn, as the choir sang: "I will be there for you, I will care. I need you, and I'm always there."

Willie Juan knew, oh, God, somehow he knew. Instinctively, he knew it was El Shaddai. Through the veil of his tears, he looked out and was shocked to see a light. He saw a light shining in the darkness. He could see. His vision had returned.

The Medicine Man walked, striding down the tear-drenched steps of the stadium with the peasants of Hopi gathered in dancing procession before him. As if moved by an irresistible force, the orchestra and choir broke into Handel's "Messiah," "King of Kings and Lord of Lords, King of Kings and Lord of Lords."

The Medicine Man reached the elevated platform, reached out, embraced Willie Juan, and kissed him on both cheeks.

"Willie Juan," Jesus said, "I needed you. For many years, the infant has been asleep in the hearts of so many men. Tonight, your faith and longing called them to life. Look out there, look around the stadium. See the faces of those men, aglow, alive. Your faith called them to life."

"O Señor, El Shaddai, I have wandered so far, gotten so lost, and nothing goes right when I don't walk with you. All I ever wanted, though I looked in the wrong places, was to find you. My life is so stale, everything is so dark and so flat when I try to walk without you."

"Willie Juan, this is my birthday. You may ask for whatever you want and it's yours."

Delirious with joy, Willie Juan stammered, "Oh, my friend, first you give me back my sight, and now you give me yourself. I dare not ask for anything more."

Jesus looked deeply and tenderly into Willie Juan's eyes. "She will be waiting for you on the porch when you return to Hopi. I have raised Ana Wim from the dead and given her back to you as a living reminder of my presence. She will cry my tears, give you my hand, show you my heart, and hold you so tight in my love.

"You will need each other, Willie Juan, as you walk hand in hand to the house of Abba. I still have many things for the two of you to do.

"Now pick up your horn."

Willie Juan picked up his horn, and Señor Jesus, the Son of Abba, El Shaddai, stood beside his friend. In a lyrical duet on their horns they played "O Holy Night" as the Infant stirred in the hearts of all the men and women, and a shower of white, yellow, lavender, and pink petals came cascading from the sky.

About the Author

In the latter days of Depression-era New York City, Brennan Manning — christened Richard Francis Xavier — was born to Emmett and Amy Manning. He grew up in Brooklyn along with his brother, Robert, and sister, Geraldine. After graduating from high school and attending St. John's University (Queens, New York) for two years, he enlisted in the U.S. Marine Corps and was sent overseas to fight in the Korean War.

Upon his return, Brennan began a program in journalism at the University of Missouri. But he departed after a semester, restlessly searching for something "more" in life. "Maybe the something 'more' is God," an advisor had suggested, triggering Brennan's enrollment in a Catholic seminary in Loretto, Pennsylvania.

In February 1956, while Brennan was meditating on the Stations of the Cross, a powerful experience of the personal love of Jesus Christ sealed the call of God on his life. "At that moment," he later recalled, "the entire Christian life became for me an intimate, heartfelt relationship with Jesus." Four years later, he graduated from St. Francis College (major in philosophy; minor in Latin) and went on to complete four years of advanced studies in theology. May 1963 marked his graduation from St. Francis Seminary and ordination to the Franciscan priesthood.

Brennan's ministry responsibilities in succeeding years took him from the hallways of academia to the byways of the poor: theology instructor and campus minister at the University of Steubenville; liturgy instructor and spiritual director at St. Francis Seminary; graduate student in creative writing at Columbia University and in Scripture and liturgy at Catholic University of America; living and working among the poor in Europe and the United States.

A two-year leave of absence from the Franciscans took Brennan to Spain in the late 1960s. He joined the Little Brothers of Jesus of Charles de Foucauld, an Order committed to an uncloistered, contemplative life among the poor — a lifestyle of days spent in manual labor and nights wrapped in silence and prayer. Among his many and varied assignments, Brennan became an *aguador* (water carrier), transporting water to rural villages via donkey and buckboard; a mason's assistant, shoveling mud and straw in the blazing Spanish heat; a dishwasher in France; a voluntary prisoner in a Swiss jail, his identity as a priest known only to the warden; a solitary contemplative secluded in a remote cave for six months in the Zaragoza desert.

During his retreat in the isolated cave, Brennan was once again powerfully convicted by the revelation of God's love in the crucified Christ. On a midwinter's night, he received this word from the Lord: "For love of you I left my Father's side. I came to you who ran from me, who fled me, who did not want to hear my name. For love of you I was covered with spit, punched and beaten, and fixed to the wood of the cross." Brennan would later reflect, "Those words are burned into my life. That night, I learned what a wise old Franciscan told me the day I joined the Order — 'Once you come to know the love of Jesus Christ, nothing else in the world will seem as beautiful or desirable.'"

The early 1970s found Brennan back in the United States as he and four other priests established an experimental community in the bustling seaport city of Bayou La Batre, Alabama. Seeking to model the primitive life of the Franciscans, the fathers settled in a house on Mississippi Bay and quietly went to work on shrimp boats, ministering to the shrimpers and their families who had drifted out of reach of the church. Next to the community house was a chapel that had been destroyed by Hurricane Camille. The fathers restored it and offered a Friday night liturgy and social event, which soon became a popular gathering and precipitated many families' return to engagement in the local church.

From Alabama, Brennan moved to Fort Lauderdale, Florida, in the mid-1970s and resumed campus ministry at Broward Community College. His successful ministry was harshly interrupted, however, when he suffered a precipitate collapse into alcoholism. Six months of treatment, culminating at the Hazelden treatment center in Minnesota, restored his health and placed him on the road to recovery.

It was at this point in his life that Brennan began writing in earnest. One book soon followed upon another as invitations for him to speak and to lead spiritual retreats multiplied exponentially. The new and renewed directions in which God's call was taking Brennan eventually led him out of the Franciscan Order.

Today, Brennan travels widely as he continues to write and preach, encouraging men and women everywhere to accept and embrace the good news of God's unconditional love in Jesus Christ.

Of Related Interest

Kim Jocelyn Dickson
GIFTS FROM THE SPIRIT
*Reflections on the Diaries and Letters
of Anne Morrow Lindbergh*

In *Gifts from the Spirit* Dickson tells how her
life has been transformed by Anne Morrow
Lindbergh's writings. Drawing from Lindbergh's diaries and including her own evoca-
tive reflections, Dickson captures the essence
of Lindbergh's spirituality and womanhood.

0-8245-2010-6, $17.95 hardcover

Paula D'Arcy
A NEW SET OF EYES
Encountering the Hidden God

Through a series of meditations and parables,
D'Arcy helps readers awaken the mind to the
presence of God, free the soul from its cher-
ished idols, and infuse the emotions with joy.
By the popular author of *Gift of the Red Bird*
and *Song for Sarah.*

0-8245-1930-2, $16.95 hardcover

crossroad

by Michael L. Lindvall

THE GOOD NEWS FROM NORTH HAVEN
A Year in the Life of a Small Town

"A debut collection of...sermon-like tales covering a year in the life of a Presbyterian minister in a small Minnesota town — by a native of Minneapolis. Alter-ego Reverend David Battles and his family have discovered in their four years of small-town life that instead of outgrowing this backwater they've become attached to its every quirk and comfort — and have themselves become a local institution along the way."   — Kirkus

0-8245-2012-2, $16.95 paperback

LEAVING NORTH HAVEN
The Further Adventures of a Small Town Pastor

This eagerly awaited sequel to the bestseller *Good News from North Haven* continues to engage readers with poignant storytelling on issues of faith.

0-8245-2013-0, $16.95 paperback

crossroad

Of Related Interest

Barbara Fiand
IN THE STILLNESS YOU WILL KNOW
Exploring the Paths of Our Ancient Belonging

Popular spirituality writer Barbara Fiand is back with a moving book inspired by the death of her dearest friend and soulmate. Shadowed by grief, Fiand uses her friend's untimely passing as the starting point for ponderings about the nature of hope and the solace that comes from the beauty of nature speaking to us.

0-8245-2650-3, $16.95 paperback

Michael Morwood
GOD IS NEAR
Trusting Our Faith

Morwood reminds us that the Christian God is closer to us than our very hearts. He seeks to counter commonly held notions — like the need to earn God's love — with the loving portrait of the Father captured in the Gospels.

0-8245-1984-1, $12.95 paperback

crossroad

Of Related Interest

Ronald Rolheiser
THE SHATTERED LANTERN
Rediscovering a Felt Presence of God

The way back to a lively faith "is not a question of finding the right answers, but of living a certain way. The existence of God, like the air we breathe, need not be proven." Rolheiser shines new light on the contemplative path of Western Christianity and offers a dynamic way forward.

0-8245-1884-5, $14.95 paperback

Please support your local bookstore,
or call 1-800-707-0670 for Customer Service.

For a free catalog, write us at

THE CROSSROAD
PUBLISHING COMPANY
481 Eighth Avenue, Suite 1550
New York, NY 10001

Visit our website at
www.crossroadpublishing.com

crossroad